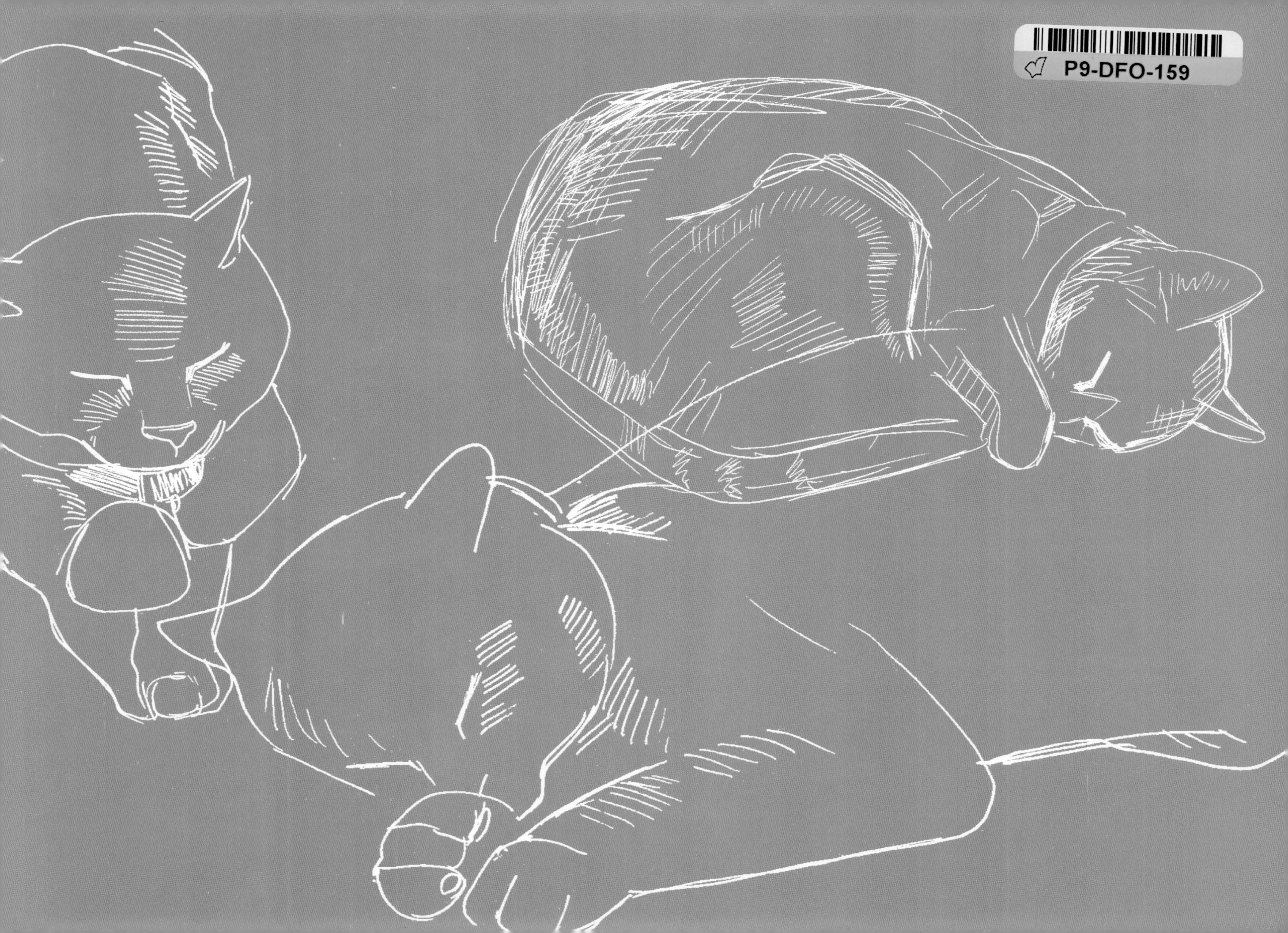

MacAdam/Cage Children's Books
155 Sansome Street, Suite 550
San Francisco, California 94104

Library of Congress Cataloging-in Publication Data

Futterer, Kurt.
[Emile. English]
Emile / written by Kurt Futterer; illustrated by Ralf Futterer; translated by Ingrid MacGillis.
p. cm.
Summary: A white cat named Emile leaves home in search of beautiful colors.
ISBN 1-931561-95-8 (hardcover : alk. paper)
[1. Color—Fiction. 2. Cats—Fiction.] I.Futterer, Ralf, ill. II. Gray, Bronwen. III. MacGillis, Sepcht. IV. MacGillis, Ingrid. V. Title.
PZ7.F96675EM 2004
[E]—dc22
2004015247
Originally published as "Emile-Eine bunte Katzengeschichte" by Futterer Eigenverlag, Germany, 1999
IBSN 3-00-004438-8 ©1999 by Futterer Eingenverlag

Illustration: Ralf Futterer
Translation: Ingrid MacGillis
Design/layout: Dirk Futterer, Angela Futterer

The author would like to give special thanks to Edward Paul Kenny and Bronwen Gray-Sepcht for their help in bringing this book to English-language readers.

Printed in Canada

Emile

Once upon a time there lived a snow-white cat named Emile. He belonged to a man and a woman. The three lived quietly together from day to day.

Yesterday, today and tomorrow.

Most of the time, Emile rested quitely in his basket.

Sometimes, he would get up and stretch this way and that way, yawn from ear to ear, and then lie down once more to sleep.

Emile was not allowed to go out, because he might get dirty.

“Besides,” said the man and the woman, “outside, there are too many dogs.”

Then, one morning, a colorful butterfly fluttered past an open window.

Emile was fascinated. “What beautiful colors!” he thought.

He just had to go outside into the world to see more of these beautiful colors.

And so he did.

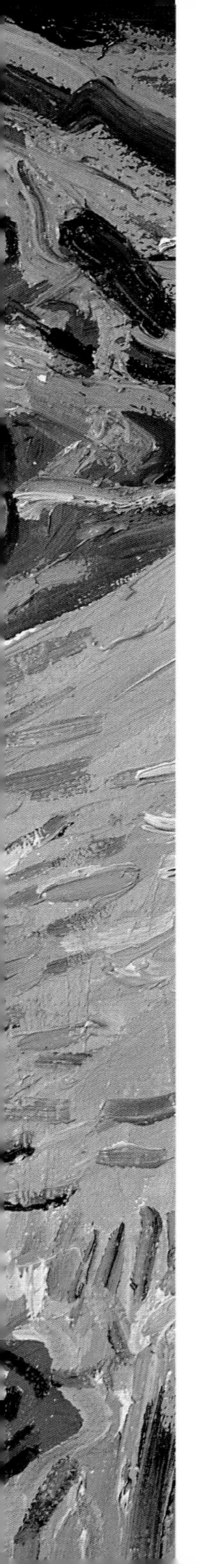

Outside, Emile met a gray
mouse. The mouse knew
she did not have to be
afraid of a cat like Emile.
"Where are you going?"
the gray mouse asked.
She was curious.
"To where life is colorful,"
replied Emile.
"Why?" asked the gray
mouse, shaking her head.
"You know you can't eat
colors! You had better
go back home!"
But Emile continued
on his way.

Emile met three kittens, playing in front of a house.

“Come inside with us!” said the first kitten.

“You will see such beautiful colors.”

“We can make believe we are painters!” said the second kitten.

“It will be so much fun!” said the third.

The idea sounded fine to Emile.

Once inside, the three kittens went crazy painting.

The house belonged to a painter named Vincent. He was amazed at what he saw. Emile was amazed too.

“Crazy,” said Vincent, over and over again, “Just crazy.”

Soon there was no stopping the kittens. Paint was everywhere. They were so excited that they even began to paint Emile's white fur. The kittens polka-dotted him with all the colors in Vincent's paint jars. Emile began to feel like a butterfly. But, at last, his thoughts turned to the man and the woman who cared for him.

"I have to go now," said Emile. "I must go home. Good-bye!"

On his way he met the little gray mouse again.

“You silly cat!” she laughed.

You and your colors have really gone too far.

Just wait and see what will happen when

you get home!”

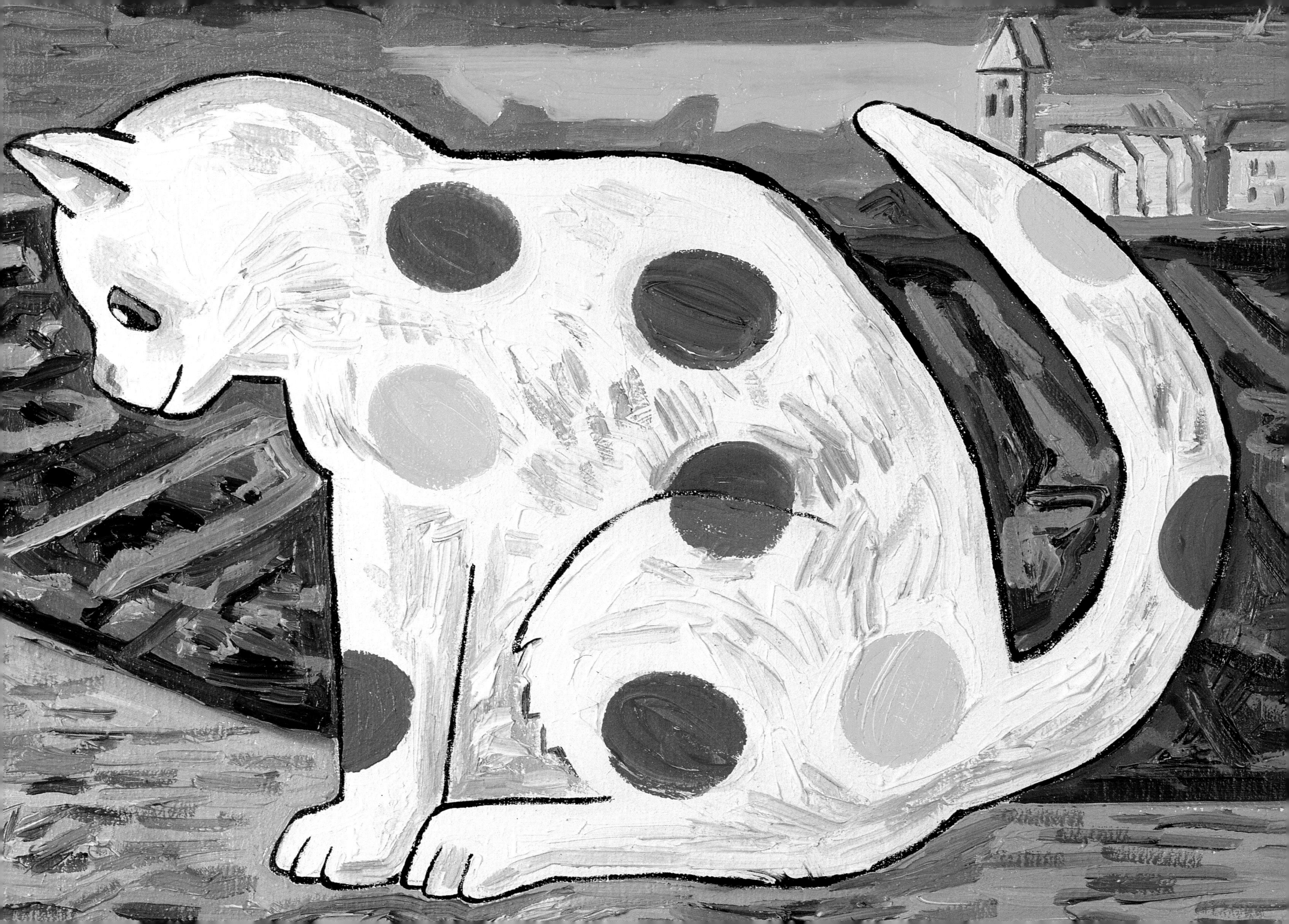

When Emile arrived home, the man and the woman were shocked.

“Oh, no…oh my goodness!” said the woman throwing her hands in the air.

“You look like such a mess!” said the man. Emile was sent to his basket without any food.

But it wasn’t long before the man and the woman relaxed and began to see Emile through different eyes.

“Doesn’t he look happier now?” asked the woman.

“We must have been really color blind,” said the man.

So they let him be and decided to like Emile just the way he was. He would even be allowed to go outside.

Emile had brought color into the house.

Now, they wanted even more color.

The woman went right out to buy flowers.

The man got brushes and paint.

They quickly got down to work. Together they painted the grayness right out of the house. In the end, all three were splattered with color. "Emile has rubbed off on us!" said the man and the woman at the very same time. This made them all laugh, and soon they were singing and dancing with joy.